Jeff Gordon

Additional Titles in the Sports Reports *Series*

Andre Agassi
Star Tennis Player
(0-89490-798-0)

Troy Aikman
Star Quarterback
(0-89490-927-4)

Roberto Alomar
Star Second Baseman
(0-7660-1079-1)

Charles Barkley
Star Forward
(0-89490-655-0)

Jeff Gordon
Star Race Car Driver
(0-7660-1083-X)

Wayne Gretzky
Star Center
(0-89490-930-4)

Ken Griffey, Jr.
Star Outfielder
(0-89490-802-2)

Scott Hamilton
Star Figure Skater
(0-7660-1236-0)

Anfernee Hardaway
Star Guard
(0-7660-1234-4)

Grant Hill
Star Forward
(0-7660-1078-3)

Michael Jordan
Star Guard
(0-89490-482-5)

Shawn Kemp
Star Forward
(0-89490-929-0)

Mario Lemieux
Star Center
(0-89490-932-0)

Karl Malone
Star Forward
(0-89490-931-2)

Dan Marino
Star Quarterback
(0-89490-933-9)

Mark McGwire
Star Home Run Hitter
(0-7660-1329-4)

Mark Messier
Star Center
(0-89490-801-4)

Reggie Miller
Star Guard
(0-7660-1082-1)

Chris Mullin
Star Forward
(0-89490-486-8)

Hakeem Olajuwon
Star Center
(0-89490-803-0)

Shaquille O'Neal
Star Center
(0-89490-656-9)

Scottie Pippen
Star Forward
(0-7660-1080-5)

Cal Ripken, Jr.
Star Shortstop
(0-89490-485-X)

David Robinson
Star Center
(0-89490-483-3)

Barry Sanders
Star Running Back
(0-89490-484-1)

Deion Sanders
Star Athlete
(0-89490-652-6)

Junior Seau
Star Linebacker
(0-89490-800-6)

Emmitt Smith
Star Running Back
(0-89490-653-4)

Frank Thomas
Star First Baseman
(0-89490-659-3)

Thurman Thomas
Star Running Back
(0-89490-445-0)

Chris Webber
Star Forward
(0-89490-799-9)

Tiger Woods
Star Golfer
(0-7660-1081-3)

Steve Young
Star Quarterback
(0-89490-654-2)

Jim Kelly
Star Quarterback
(0-89490-446-9)

Jerry Rice
Star Wide Receiver
(0-89490-928-2)

SPORTS REPORTS

Jeff Gordon

Star Race Car Driver

Paul Steenkamer

Enslow Publishers, Inc.

40 Industrial Road
Box 398
Berkeley Heights, NJ 07922
USA

PO Box 38
Aldershot
Hants GU12 6BP
UK

http://www.enslow.com

Library of Congress Cataloging-in-Publication Data

Steenkamer, Paul.
Jeff Gordon: star race car driver / Paul Steenkamer.
p. cm. — (Sports reports)
Includes bibliographical references (p.) and index.
Summary: Discusses the racing career, life, and accomplishments of the youngest driver to win the Winston Cup title.
ISBN 0-7660-1083-X
1. Gordon, Jeff, 1971- —Juvenile literature. 2. Automobile racing drivers—United States—Biography—Juvenile literature. [1. Gordon, Jeff, 1971- . 2. Automobile racing drivers.] I. Title. II. Series.
GV1032.G67S836 1999
796.72'092—dc21
[B] 98-36497
CIP
AC

Printed in the United States of America

10 9 8 7 6 5 4 3

To Our Readers:
All Internet addresses in this book were active and appropriate when we went to press. Any comments or suggestions can be sent by e-mail to Comments@enslow.com or to the address on the back cover.

Photo Credits: Archive Photos, pp. 36, 56; Courtesy Performance PR Plus, Inc., pp. 33, 43, 58; © Dave Hill Photography, p. 24; Reuters/Joe Skipper/Archive Photos, pp. 12, 64, 88; Reuters/Karl Ronstrom/Archive Photos, p. 26; Reuters/Pierre DuCharme/Archive Photos, pp. 16, 18; Reuters/Robin Jerstad/Archive Photos, p. 46; Reuters/Winston Luzier/Archive Photos, pp. 11, 38, 48, 67, 72, 80.

Cover Photo: Courtesy of Performance PR Plus, Inc.

Contents

1 The Daytona 500 7

2 NASCAR Racing Basics 14

3 Kid Racer 21

4 Busch Grand National Racing . . . 28

5 Victory Lane 35

6 The Brickyard 400 44

7 Refuse to Lose 53

8 Defending Champion 66

9 Six Million-Dollar Man. 78

Chapter Notes. 91

Career Statistics. 99

Where to Write 101

Index 103

Chapter 1

The Daytona 500

There was still one thing Jeff Gordon had not done after only four seasons in the National Association of Stock Car Auto Racing (NASCAR) Winston Cup Series. By 1997, twenty-five-year-old Gordon had already won nineteen races. He had been named 1993 Rookie of the Year and had won the 1995 Winston Cup Championship. But Gordon had not won NASCAR's biggest race, the Daytona 500.

Racing in third place midway through the 1997 Daytona 500, Gordon was in trouble. Coming out of turn one, he began to lose control of his car. He hung on and narrowly avoided hitting the wall. Sensing he had a problem with one of his tires, Gordon radioed crew chief Ray Evernham to get ready. He was coming into the pit. The pit stop would have to be fast to keep Gordon in the race. During the pit stop Gordon's crew, nicknamed the "Rainbow Warriors" (because of the rainbow stripes across the hood of Gordon's car and on the front of their uniforms), changed one of the car's rear tires. The tire had been cut by wreckage on the track. Gordon zoomed back onto the track in thirty-first, just in front of race leader Mark Martin, but he was still on the lead lap. Gordon was now running the race of his life to keep from being lapped. If Martin managed to pass him, any chance for his first Daytona 500 victory would end.

For the next several laps Gordon battled Martin, blocking all attempts to be passed. All he could do was hang on and hope for a caution flag that would allow him to go to the back of the pack of cars on the lead lap. After holding Martin off for eleven laps, Gordon got the break he needed. The cars driven by Greg Sacks and Jeff Burton collided. The collision left debris on the track and brought out the yellow caution flag. Said Gordon: "When you have a tire going down and are able to get a good one and not lose a lap, and when you're sitting there with the lead pack about to lap you and you get a caution, those are signs to you that it's your day."[1] Having been given a second chance, Gordon was determined to make the most of it. Following the caution that kept him in the race, Gordon found himself at the back of the lead pack with almost half the race left. When the green flag flew again, Gordon stepped on the accelerator and began weaving his Chevrolet Monte Carlo in and out of traffic. With twenty laps to go in the 200-lap race, he was in third. But, racing between him and leader Bill Elliott was NASCAR superstar Dale Earnhardt.

In the weeks leading up to the race, all the talk was about Dale Earnhardt. Despite winning an amazing seven Winston Cup Championships in his career, Earnhardt had yet to win NASCAR's biggest race. "It's the Daytona 500," he said after a heartbreaking near miss a few years ago. "I'm not supposed to win the thing."[2] Earnhardt had seventy Winston Cup victories, but he was 0 for 18 in the Daytona 500 entering the 1997 race. Keeping things in perspective, Earnhardt noted, "It's an important race, but there are lots of races left to run."[3]

FACT

The first Daytona 500 was held in 1949 on a makeshift course carved out on the beach. Red Byron won the race. The Daytona International Speedway opened in 1959. Lee Petty won the first Daytona 500 held there. Today, the Daytona 500 is run on the same speedway.

Earnhardt was racing hard as he went for his first Daytona 500 victory in nineteen tries. Gordon raced behind Earnhardt for nine laps. Then, with eleven laps to go, he made his move. Racing out of turn two, Gordon sped his Chevrolet up close to the left rear of Earnhardt's car. The momentum from Gordon's car shifted the airflow around Earnhardt's car. This caused Earnhardt to lose control. At 180 miles per hour, that can be a problem. Earnhardt was already riding high on the track. Gordon's move caused him to bump the wall. Earnhardt's car then came down the track and hit the side of Gordon's car. Gordon was able to keep control of his car and continue racing. Earnhardt was forced to let off the gas pedal. As Earnhardt slowed, the speeding cars of Dale Jarrett and Ernie Irvan had nowhere to go. Jarrett hit Earnhardt from behind. The collision caused Earnhardt's car to turn sideways. Then Irvan broadsided Earnhardt. Earnhardt's number 3 car rolled over onto its side. The crash ended Earnhardt's chance to win the Daytona 500.

Said Earnhardt,

> Gordon was on the inside of me and got up against me tight. My car scuffed the wall a little bit. I got back into him and checked off the throttle. Somebody behind me turned me, and when it turned sideways it started going on its top.[4]

When the caution flag was lifted following the wreck, Gordon was in second place, trailing Bill Elliott. Gordon's Hendrick Motorsports teammates, Terry Labonte and Ricky Craven, were behind him in third and fourth. "With three Hendrick cars behind you, you don't have a chance," Elliott said after the race. "I was dead meat, and I knew it. It

FACT

The National Association of Stock Car Auto Racing (NASCAR), was formed in December 1947 in Daytona Beach, Florida, to combine the existing stock car racing leagues. Bill France was NASCAR's first president. Red Byron won the first season title in 1949.

Jeff Gordon (left) is shown here talking to Hendrick Motorsports teammate Terry Labonte.

was just a matter of when and where."[5] Gordon made his move for the lead on lap 194, heading into turn one.

After radioing each of his teammates to see whether they were with him, Gordon drove down below Elliott in turn one. Elliott cut down the track to try to block Gordon. As Elliott attempted to block Gordon's move, Labonte and Craven went high. Elliott nearly forced Gordon into the infield, but all three cars made the pass. "I had a ton of momentum from Terry and Ricky," Gordon said. "Bill knew I was going low. But I kept going lower and lower to see just how low he wanted to go to block me. Hey,

Jeff Gordon celebrates after winning NASCAR's biggest race—the Daytona 500. At just twenty-five years old, Gordon was the youngest driver to win the Daytona 500.

I would've gone . . . to the infield if that's what it took. I was going by, no matter what."[6]

Gordon, Labonte, and Craven were racing one, two, and three when a multicar crash occurred on lap 196. With just four laps to go, the race would end under caution. There would be no dash to the finish between these teammates. The Hendrick Motorsports team finished an unprecedented first, second, and third. Jeff Gordon had won NASCAR's biggest race in only his fifth attempt. At twenty-five, he broke Richard Petty's record as the youngest driver to win the Daytona 500.

Winning the Daytona 500 left Gordon speechless. "It's hard to explain what this means to me," Gordon said. "You don't know how big Daytona is until you win it."[7]

Chapter 2

NASCAR Racing Basics

Not sure what drafting is or what the white flag means? Like all sports, NASCAR racing has its own unique rules and vocabulary. This chapter contains information to help you better understand NASCAR racing and the phrases that appear in this book.

Draft and Drafting

Draft. Draft refers to the airflow around a car as it races around the track. Because of the incredible speeds at which stock cars race, they encounter strong wind resistance.

Drafting. A driver who is drafting drives up close to the bumper of the car in front. By doing this, the driver is pushing the car in front and also being sucked into the lead car's airflow, or draft. This action helps both cars go faster. In addition, because the car in front is pushing against the wind, the car following uses less gas to maintain the same speed as the car ahead of it. A driver pulling out of the draft gets a boost from the lead car. In short, a sling-shot effect is created. This makes passing easier.

Flags

Green Flag. The green flag signals the drivers to start racing. It is waved at the start of the race and at all restarts.

Yellow Flag. During the race, NASCAR officials wave the yellow flag (also called the caution flag) to inform drivers of problems on the track, such as a wreck, debris or oil on the track, or a disabled car. When the yellow flag is out, known as a caution period, drivers must reduce their speed. They also cannot pass each other. Track position is determined by the position in which drivers cross the start/finish line at the end of the current lap.

Although drivers are not allowed to pass during a caution period, they can bunch up behind the car ahead of them. So, if the race leader was ahead of the second- place car by half a lap before the caution, when the caution is over, the second car will be right behind the leader.

To end a caution period, NASCAR officials wave

the green flag. This lets drivers know they can resume racing.

Red Flag. The red flag signals drivers to stop racing. This flag is waved only when there is a serious accident on the track or in the event of rain.

Black Flag. The black flag signals that a driver has broken a rule, such as speeding on pit road. When a driver is black flagged, NASCAR officials notify the team's crew chief of the penalty by radio. The driver is penalized for a certain amount of time (depending on the severity of the rule broken).

White Flag. The white flag indicates that there is only one lap remaining in the race.

Checkered Flag. When the race leader completes the final lap, NASCAR officials wave the checkered flag.

The red flag is waved only when a serious accident (such as the one shown here) occurs or in the event of rain.

The checkered flag signals the end of the race for all cars on the track, regardless of whether or not they have completed all laps. In this way, drivers may finish one, two, or more laps down (behind the winner).

Lapped

If the race leader is more than one lap ahead of a slower car, the slower car is lapped. A car that has been lapped once would have to pass the leader twice to take the lead.

NASCAR Divisions

NASCAR has twelve racing divisions. They are the Winston Cup Series, Busch Grand National Series, Craftsman Truck Series, Winston Racing Series, Winston West Series, Featherlite Modified Tour, Busch North Series, Goody's Dash Series, Slim Jim All-Pro Series, REB-CO Northwest Tour, Featherlite Southwest Tour, and the Busch All-Star Tour. The Winston Cup is the top division. Drivers in this division race in front of the largest crowds for the most prize money.

The Winston Cup season begins in February with the Daytona 500 in Daytona Beach, Florida. The season ends in November at the Atlanta Motor Speedway in Georgia. During the season, the drivers race nearly every week. Most racetracks host two Winston Cup races each year. For example, the

Daytona International Speedway hosts the Daytona 500 in February and the Pepsi 400 in July.

In addition to regular Winston Cup races, NASCAR also holds two all-star races each year—the Bud Shootout (previously the Busch Clash) and the Winston.

The Pit

Each driver has a pit stop along pit road. The pit is where the driver's crew is stationed. Drivers go into the pit when they need gas or new tires, when there is a problem with their car, or when the black flag is raised.

Qualifying

Before each race, NASCAR holds a qualifying event. One at a time, each driver completes one lap. The

The checkered flag (being waved in the foreground) signals the end of the race for all cars on the track. Here, Jeff Gordon, in car number 24 edges out teammate Terry LaBonte in car number 5.

driver who posts the fastest time for that lap starts the race in first. The first starting position is called the pole position, or simply "the pole." The other drivers fill in the remaining starting positions in descending order, according to their qualifying time.

The Daytona 500 is the only race that determines starting positions differently. For the Daytona 500, the first two starting positions go to the drivers who post the fastest qualifying lap. The remaining starting positions are determined through two 125-mile qualifying races. The drivers are split into two groups, and the qualifying races are held on the Thursday before the race. Starting positions for the qualifying races are determined by a traditional qualifying lap.

Stock Cars

When NASCAR was created, its founders decided that the cars raced should resemble what Americans drove (stock cars). In this way, people could relate to the cars being raced. Stock car racing is the only major form of track racing that is restricted to American-made automobiles. Although stock cars may look like cars driven on the open road, they are far from your typical car. Stock cars have a driver's seat only, no doors, a great deal of safety equipment, and very powerful engines. These cars can reach speeds of 200 miles (320 kilometers) per hour.

Tight and Loose

Tight and loose are terms that drivers use to describe how their car is handling. If a car is tight, the car's front end pulls toward the outside wall. This pulling will require the driver to oversteer to the left.

If a car is loose, it does not respond well when the driver turns the steering wheel. The rear of the car slides up toward the wall when the car speeds through turns.

Victory Lane

After the race, the winner drives into victory lane. Victory lane is usually in the infield of the racetrack. NASCAR presents the check and trophy to its winning driver here. The winning driver also poses for pictures in victory lane.

Chapter 3

Kid Racer

In 1971, NASCAR legend Richard Petty, then thirty-three years old, won his third Daytona 500 and his third Winston Cup Championship. That same year, on August 4, Jeffrey Michael Gordon was born in Vallejo, California.

Jeff's early years were not typical. His mom and dad divorced when he was a baby. He and his older sister, Kim, lived with their mother, Carol. By the time of Jeff's first birthday, his mom had begun dating John Bickford, a coworker. Bickford worked in the auto parts business and race cars were his hobby. Before long, Jeff's mom and John Bickford were married.

By age four, Jeff learned to ride a bicycle. Like many of the other kids in his neighborhood, he also began bicycle motocross racing (BMX). BMX races are held on dirt tracks that have many bumps and sharp turns and are less than a quarter mile long. BMX bicycles have small wheels and wide tires to help prevent riders from slipping in the turns. Riders wear full helmets and padded clothing for protection against falls (which frequently occur). Jeff attended a few BMX events. But his mom quickly disapproved of the dangerous sport. "At BMX events they were hauling kids away in ambulances all the time," said Jeff's mom.[1]

Jeff's mother's disapproval of BMX racing did not put an end to his early racing career. At age five, his stepfather brought home a quarter-midget race car. A quarter-midget race car has an open-cockpit design, like the larger midget car or sprint car. The driver is protected by a roll cage, seat belt and harness, and helmet. A quarter-midget car runs on a fuel called methanol and can generate from 3 to 12 horsepower.

At first, Jeff's mom was shocked by the idea of racing quarter-midgets. "But," she said, "it didn't take long to realize that it was a lot safer than the bikes."[2] Jeff loved driving his little race car. So, his stepfather created a makeshift track for him in a field near their home. "We'd take that car out every night after I got home from work and run it lap after lap," recalled Jeff's stepfather. "Jeff couldn't seem to get enough of it."[3]

Soon after Jeff began practicing in the quarter-midget race car, he began competing in local races. Jeff displayed natural talent. He was soon racing as often as possible. Said his stepfather, "Most kids in quarter-midgets race maybe twenty times a year. We raced fifty-two weekends a year, somewhere in the U.S. We had eight or nine cars. We practiced two or three times a week."[4] In 1979, after racing for just three years, eight-year-old Jeff Gordon won his first national championship in the quarter-midget division. With that championship, the legend of Jeff Gordon began.

After winning the 1979 quarter-midget championship, Jeff moved up to racing 10-horsepower go-carts. He was competing against older, more experienced drivers and winning regularly. He alternated between racing go-carts and quarter-midgets over the next several years. He won his second quarter-midget national championship at age ten. By age twelve, having raced fifty-two weekends a year since age five, he had won more than two hundred races. But he started to burn out.

"I started getting tired of it," said Gordon. "So we took off that summer and started going to a lake. We got a ski boat and I started water skiing. I really got into it. But I was ready to race again before long. By next summer, we sold the ski boat. I started driving sprint cars."[5]

A sprint car is a thousand-pound beast. It can generate anywhere from 650 to 800 horsepower and can reach speeds of 100 miles per hour or more. Sprint cars have the same open-cockpit design as quarter-midget or midget cars. They also have two wings on top to help prevent the car from rolling over. Sprint car racing is considered one of the most dangerous forms of racing.

Drivers of sprint cars in California have to be at least sixteen years old. Jeff's family realized his talent and wanted to provide him with new

Sprint cars, such as the one shown here, weigh about one thousand pounds and can reach speeds of 100 miles per hour or more.

challenges. So they moved to Pittsboro, Indiana. In the Midwest, there was no minimum age requirement for racing sprint cars. As Jeff told it, "Nobody was fool enough to drive that young, so they didn't think they needed an age rule."[6]

Living in Pittsboro, Jeff was fifteen minutes away from one of the most famous places in auto racing—the Indianapolis Motor Speedway. One of Jeff's dreams was to race an Indy car in the Indianapolis 500. Indy cars have one seat, an open cockpit, open wheels, and a sleek fiberglass body. The cars' engines burn a form of alcohol called methanol, which provides maximum horsepower without overheating the engine. Indy car races are held on oval asphalt tracks and on road courses. Races range from 150 to 500 miles long. Indy cars can average more than 200 miles per hour on an oval track.

FACT

Richard Petty holds the following records in NASCAR's Winston Cup: wins (200), wins in a single season (27), consecutive races won (10), top-five finishes (555), top-ten finishes (712), poles (126), laps led (52,194), races led (599), career starts (1,184), and consecutive years racing (35).

Jeff raced sprint cars all over the Midwest. In 1987, at age sixteen, he became the youngest driver ever granted a United States Auto Club (USAC) license. That same year, Jeff won sixteen sprint car races. By age eighteen, Jeff was competing on the USAC sprint car circuit. He continued racing full midgets, too, and became the youngest driver to win the USAC Midget Series Championship.

During this time, Jeff attended Tri-West High

School in Pittsboro. He also raced as much as possible. Racing, however, took its toll on Jeff's social life. He did not play any sports in school. His friends were the other racers he competed against. "I never really had much of a best friend," recalled Gordon. "Most of my time was spent racing, so I did miss out on some of the things the other kids did. But I never have regretted it."[7]

Jeff skipped both his junior and senior proms. On graduation night, instead of celebrating with his classmates, Jeff was racing.

After high school, Jeff had to decide what he was going to do with his life. He discussed his future with his mother and stepfather. They decided that

The first time Jeff Gordon sat behind the wheel of a stock car (such as the ones shown here racing at the Daytona 500), he knew he wanted to race.

breaking into the Indy car circuit was too hard because Indy car drivers had to come up with their own sponsors. "To me, that was a lost cause," said Gordon. "So my stepfather made some connections and enrolled me in driving schools all over the country."[8]

The first time Jeff sat behind the wheel of a stock car and took it onto the track, he knew what he wanted to do. "That first day, the first time I got in a stock car," Gordon recalled, "I said, 'This is it. This is what I want to do.' The car was different from anything that I was used to. It was so big and heavy. It felt very fast but very smooth. I loved it."[9]

By enrolling him in driving schools, his parents hoped that Gordon would get noticed by a stock car team owner. One of those schools was the Buck Baker NASCAR Driving School in Rockingham, North Carolina. The plan worked. At the Buck Baker school, Jeff was noticed by team owner Hugh Connerly.

Connerly entered Gordon in his first Busch Grand National race, the level below Winston Cup, in the fall of 1990. Jeff Gordon was just nineteen years old. He qualified second for the race and ran well before crashing. He was not hurt.

Jeff had his first opportunity to race a stock car in a Busch Grand National race, and was eager to try again.

FACT

Roger Penske is a famous race car owner. His teams have won the Indianapolis 500 ten times. Famous drivers that have driven for him include Bobby Unser, Mario Andretti, Tom Sneva, and Rick Mears. Although Penske is thought of as an Indy-car owner, he also owns Rusty Wallace's Winston Cup team.

Chapter 4

Busch Grand National Racing

Jeff Gordon joined Bill Davis's Ford team for the 1991 NASCAR Busch Grand National season. He drove the white number 1 Baby Ruth car. He did well and gained valuable experience racing stock cars. He did not win any races, but he was named the Busch Grand National Rookie of the Year. His best finish that year was second. That finish was in the Granger Select 400 at the Hickory Motor Speedway in North Carolina. Gordon also continued to race sprint cars and became the youngest driver to win the USAC Silver Crown Division Championship.

Jeff Gordon had gotten used to driving a stock car and competing in the Busch series in 1991. Twenty-year-old Jeff Gordon was ready to go in

1992. Early in the season, Gordon tied a Busch Grand National record when he captured his third pole in a row. But he still had not won a race. Then, on Saturday, March 15, 1992, at the Atlanta Motor Speedway, Gordon broke through.

He overcame a mistake to win. He started the race on the pole. But he ran into trouble on lap 68 of the 197-lap race. His car began to run out of gas. Gordon and his crew had miscalculated how far he could go on the gas in his car. It looked like that mistake would cost him a chance to win. But someone was looking out for Gordon. Just as his car began slowing down, the engine went on Robert Huffman's Buick. This brought out a caution flag. Gordon coasted into the pits and refueled. When he resumed the race, he was in twenty-third place, but he was still on the lead lap. If the caution flag had not come out, Gordon would have been lapped. Winning would have been impossible.

Gordon was given a second chance, and he made the most of it. He weaved his way through the field until he reached the leaders. Then, on lap 162, he passed veteran NASCAR driver Dale Jarrett to take the lead. After taking the lead, Gordon did not look back. "With about 20 laps to go, I was about to get choked up," he said. "I was so worried that something was going to happen. I prayed, please don't let it."[1] It didn't.

Gordon's second Busch series victory was even sweeter. On the day before the Champion 300, NASCAR superstar Dale Earnhardt came up to Gordon and gave him a little pressure. As Gordon told the story, "He came up to me and said, 'Boy, you got your car running 32.50s [32.50 seconds per lap] consistently?' I said, 'No.' He said, 'You'd better, because I'm going to run you down and blow you away.'"[2]

On race day Gordon was prepared for the challenge. When he passed Earnhardt, he turned and gave him a friendly wave. Next, Gordon set his sights on front-runner Dick Trickle.

Trickle did his best to keep Gordon from taking the lead. He shifted his car to block Gordon. Then, heading into the third turn with thirty-eight laps to go, the two leaders came upon a lapped car. Gordon used the lapped car and made his move. He drove alongside the rear of Trickle's car, which was blocked by the lapped car. This caused Trickle's car and the lapped car to drift up the track. Gordon zoomed underneath. Trickle steered back down trying to stop Gordon, causing their cars to collide. Gordon held on to win the race. "I didn't call it a pass, I called it a slam," Gordon said afterward. "I saw the opportunity and I went for it. Luckily it turned out all right."[3]

In October, Gordon won the All Pro 300 at the Charlotte Motor Speedway. It was Gordon's final victory of the season, and it was won by narrowly avoiding disaster.

Gordon charged into the lead on lap 146 of the 200-lap race. He built an impressive 10.6-second lead by lap 182. He was in great position to win his third race of the year. Then a tire blew on Joe Nemechek's car. Nemechek's trouble brought out the yellow caution flag. The caution allowed the cars to bunch up, eliminating Gordon's large lead. When the caution was lifted, Gordon was battling Michael Waltrip for the win. Then, with four laps to go, everything changed. Five cars crashed in turn four, where Gordon and Waltrip were heading. The crash brought out the final caution of the day. Whoever crossed the finish line first after this lap would win the race under caution. Gordon learned of the situation this way. "My spotter told me, I hate to tell you this, but there are cars all over the track and you're going to have to race back."[4]

The two cars sped toward the remnants of the wreck as they dueled for the finish line. As they came through the scene of the crash, Waltrip went low and Gordon went high. Unfortunately for

Gordon, Robert Pressley's damaged car was slowly heading backward up to the wall in his path. Gordon pushed the gas pedal on his Ford to the floor and held his breath. "I can't believe I made it," Gordon said later. "It was incredibly close. I saw my life pass before my eyes. You couldn't have put a piece of paper between mine and Robert's car nor between my car and the wall. I held my breath until I got all the way back to the first turn because I still wasn't sure I'd made it."[5]

FACT

Henry Ford founded the Ford Motor Company in 1903. The company began with approximately ten employees working in a small garage in Detroit. Today, the Ford Motor Company is the world's second-largest producer of cars and trucks, employing more than 370,000 people in thirty countries.

Gordon crossed the finish line first. He took the checkered flag under caution for his third victory of the year. The win and the $72,080 payday helped Gordon break the Busch Grand National season record for winnings.

Gordon set another Busch Grand National record when he captured his eleventh pole of the season at the AC Delco 200 in October. Gordon not only captured the pole, but also broke the track record. On his record-breaking eleventh pole, Gordon said, "I'll be honest, today we were going for the record. When we came in here and tested, we tested real well. When we got here today, the car was a rocket right off the truck. We've been waiting on this record all day long."[6]

Gordon's terrific 1992 Busch Grand National season did not go unnoticed. Early in the year, Winston

When Winston Cup team owner Rick Hendrick spotted Jeff Gordon (shown here), Gordon was racing in a Busch Grand National race in Atlanta, Georgia.

Cup team owner Rick Hendrick spotted Gordon. He was racing in a Busch Grand National race in Atlanta. "I caught this white car racing out of the corner of my eye," Hendrick recalled. "As it went into the corner, I could see that it was extremely loose. I said, 'Man, that guy's going to wreck! You just can't drive a car that loose.' But the car went on to win the race."[7] That white car was driven by twenty-year-old sensation Jeff Gordon.

FACT

Eleuthere Irenee duPont de Nemours, a French immigrant, founded the DuPont Company in 1802. DuPont began as a producer of gunpowder. Its first gunpowder works was located just outside Wilmington, Delaware. Today, DuPont is one of the world's largest chemical companies. DuPont inventions include Kevlar, Lycra, Mylar, Nylon, SilverStone, Stainmaster, Teflon, and Tyvek.

Not long after his first Busch series victory at the Atlanta Motor Speedway, Gordon signed a deal with Hendrick. Gordon would drive the number 24, rainbow-striped, DuPont Automotive Finishes Chevrolet. He would make his Winston Cup debut as soon as the 1992 Busch Grand National season was complete. The Busch season ended before the Winston Cup season, so Gordon's first Winston Cup race would be the final race of the 1992 season. The race would be run at the same Atlanta racetrack where he caught the eye of team owner Rick Hendrick.

In an interesting twist of fate, Gordon's first race would be Richard Petty's last. Petty, the "king" of stock car racing, was retiring at the end of the 1992 Winston Cup season.

Chapter 5

Victory Lane

Jeff Gordon prepared for his NASCAR Winston Cup debut at the end of the 1992 season. Meanwhile, all eyes were on retiring superstar Richard Petty. Gordon qualified twenty-first for his first race and finished a distant thirty-first. But, with his first Winston Cup race under his belt, Gordon would be ready to go in 1993.

Gordon started his first full Winston Cup season with a bang. He was racing in one of the two 125-mile qualifying races for the first race of the season—the Daytona 500. Gordon's instruction from crew chief Ray Evernham was simple: qualify for the most famous stock car race of them all. Gordon, however, was not content to just make the field. He zoomed through the cars in his qualifying

Jeff Gordon's first NASCAR race at the end of the 1992 season was also the last race for Richard Petty (shown here). Petty, the king of stock car racing, retired at the end of the 1992 season.

race until he found himself in second, behind Bill Elliott. Kyle Petty was in third. Petty made his move for the lead, and Gordon seized the opportunity. He also made an attempt to get around Elliott's car. Both cars made the pass, and Gordon held off Petty to take the lead. After taking the lead, he never looked back. Gordon took the checkered flag for the victory. In doing so, he became the youngest driver to win a Daytona qualifying race.

In victory lane, while Gordon was celebrating his win, he caught the eye of Brooke Sealey. Sealey was one of the Miss Winston models at the race. Miss Winston models appear in victory lane at each race and make special appearances to promote NASCAR.

There is an unwritten rule that Miss Winstons are not to date drivers. However, Gordon and Sealey began seeing each other shortly after their meeting in victory lane. The two dated secretly for the rest of the season. They were careful not to let anyone involved in NASCAR's Winston Cup know of their relationship. Gordon and Sealey finally revealed that they were a couple at the season-ending awards banquet in New York City.

The following February, one year after their fateful meeting in victory lane, Gordon proposed. The two were married in November 1994.

FACT

Three generations of Pettys have raced in the Winston Cup. Lee Petty raced for sixteen years in the number 42 car. Lee's son, Richard, raced for thirty-five years in the number 43 car. Richard's son, Kyle, began racing in the Winston Cup in 1979. He continues to race today in the number 44 car.

Talking about her husband, Brooke Gordon said,

> When I first met Jeff I thought he would be very arrogant and think that he had everything in his grasp, but he was the total opposite. He was so sweet and genuinely nice and kind of shy. I knew from the first day that he was something really special.[1]

Gordon's winning one of the two qualifying races for the Daytona 500 allowed him to start the race third. When the race began, Gordon was ready. He quickly drove his rainbow-striped Chevrolet into the lead. He led the pack around the track and became the first rookie to lead the first lap of the Daytona 500. He ran well and battled up or near the

Jeff and Brooke Gordon (shown here) were married in November 1994, after a year of dating in secret.

front all day. His fifth-place finish was the best ever for a rookie in the Daytona 500.

Gordon raced well in 1993. He did not win any races, but he had seven top-five finishes, including two second-place finishes.

Toward the end of his first full season on the Winston Cup circuit, Gordon said, "We would sure like to win one, but we're getting experience and learning every time out. We keep doing what we're doing and we're gonna win one someday."[2] Jeff Gordon finished fourteenth in the final Winston Cup standings. He was named the 1993 NASCAR Winston Cup Rookie of the Year.

He began the 1994 season by winning the Busch Clash all-star race at Daytona. The series traveled to Charlotte at the end of May for the 1994 Coca-Cola 600. Gordon was still looking for his first win in a regular Winston Cup race.

Gordon had raced well at Charlotte in the past. He won two Busch Grand National races there and his only Winston Cup pole in 1993. When qualifying began for the 1994 Coca-Cola 600, he was confident. He captured the pole for the race for the second year in a row. Talking about his qualifying lap, Gordon said, "You never know what the track's going to do until you drive it off into the corner. I went down in there hard, then jumped right back into the gas, and it stuck like glue. I had a big smile all the way down the backstretch."[3]

Making Gordon's qualifying lap all the more impressive was the fact that he had crashed his best car three days earlier, racing in the Winston Select Open. Gordon's car was damaged when he was caught up in an accident with Dale Earnhardt and Rusty Wallace. The accident caused damage to the car's front end and sides. Gordon was able to finish the race, but his car needed extensive repairs before it would be capable of racing at top form.

The Rainbow Warriors worked night and day to repair the car. After capturing the pole, Gordon gave the credit to his crew. "I owe this pole to my crew, for sure. The car may be even better than it was before the wreck. They worked in shifts to get it ready. Ray told me that they finished at 2 A.M. this morning."[4] But team owner Rick Hendrick left no doubt who the real hero was: "Most of the credit goes to the guy in the driver's seat."[5]

After capturing his first pole of the 1994 season, Gordon could feel his luck changing. "We're close to taking the checkers," he said. "We're not that far off, I guarantee you."[6]

Gordon began the race in first. With thirty laps to go, however, he was in third. He was trailing two experienced Winston Cup drivers—1989 Winston

Cup champion Rusty Wallace and Geoff Bodine. Gordon was participating in only his forty-ninth Winston Cup race. He needed a miracle to capture his first victory.

As the leaders sped toward the finish, Gordon waited for an opportunity. They had been racing for more than five hundred miles under the lights at the Charlotte Motor Speedway. Wallace, Bodine, and Gordon would each need to stop in the pits one last time for new tires and gas.

Rusty Wallace was the first of the leaders to come into the pits. He gave up the lead on lap 375. There were only twenty-five laps to go in the 400-lap race. Wallace's pit crew put four new tires on his car and filled it up with gas. His pit stop took 17.22 seconds. Geoff Bodine drove into the pits next, on lap 379. In a pit stop lasting 17.98 seconds, he also got four new tires and gas. Gordon had the lead after Bodine went into the pits, but Gordon would have to stop in the pits, too.

Gordon drove his rainbow-striped Chevrolet into the pits on lap 382. He went into the pits after Wallace and Bodine on purpose. He and crew chief Ray Evernham had a plan. If it worked, it would carry Gordon to victory lane. After watching both Wallace and Bodine stop and get four new tires and a full tank of gas, the Rainbow Warriors changed only the two right-side tires. They added only a half tank of gas. The pit stop took a speedy 8.65 seconds.

Gordon and Evernham were taking a chance. If one of the two old tires on the car wore out or if the car ran out of gas, the race would end in disappointment. But if the gamble worked, the time saved in the pits would carry Gordon to his first Winston Cup victory.

Gordon resumed racing in second, trailing Ricky Rudd. But Rudd also had to stop in the pits before the end of the race or his car would run out of gas. Finally, on lap 391, Rudd turned down pit road. As Rudd headed into the pits, Gordon took charge of the race. With less than ten laps to go, Jeff Gordon, racing with only two new tires, began to pull away. "I knew I had the race with 10 laps to go as long as I didn't mess up," said Gordon.[7]

Gordon drove hard all the way to the finish. He extended his lead on each lap. Then, after racing 600 grueling miles, Jeff Gordon took his first checkered flag. Just twenty-two years old, Gordon was the second-youngest driver to win a NASCAR Winston Cup Series race.

In victory lane, Gordon talked about what the win meant to him. "This is the highlight of my life," he said. "If there is a feeling any higher than this, I don't know what it is."[8]

After a year and a half in NASCAR's top series, the Winston Cup, Jeff Gordon captured a win.

After the race, veteran NASCAR drivers spoke about the young man who had stolen the race. Second-place finisher Rusty Wallace said,

> I never thought he'd try two tires, and I never thought it would work. Looking back, in hindsight, we should have changed two (instead of four), and we would have won by a ton. His gamble worked. You have to give it to him because that is what this sport is all about.[9]

Third-place finisher Geoff Bodine said, "Jeff held us off after changing two tires and I can't believe it. I thought for sure Rusty would catch him.[10]

Jeff Gordon had been racing cars and winning since the age of five. Now, he had finally reached the top. After a year and a half in NASCAR's top series, he had finally made it into victory lane.

Chapter 6

The Brickyard 400

Between 1911 and 1993, the only auto race run at the Indianapolis Motor Speedway was the Indianapolis 500, an Indy car race. Among race car drivers and fans, the Indianapolis Motor Speedway is known simply as "the brickyard."

Jeff Gordon attended high school in nearby Pittsboro, Indiana. He was no different from other young racers. His dream growing up was to race in and win the Indianapolis 500. But Gordon realized how difficult breaking into the Indy car circuit would be. So, he found his calling racing stock cars. By choosing a career racing stock cars, Gordon thought that his dreams of returning to Indiana and racing at the Indianapolis Motor Speedway would never come to be.

Then, on April 4, 1993, the unthinkable happened in the world of racing. Tony George, president of the Indianapolis Motor Speedway, and Bill France, Jr., president of NASCAR, announced the union between the two. The inaugural NASCAR race at the Indianapolis Motor Speedway would be held in August 1994. It would be called the Brickyard 400. When ticket sales were announced for the inaugural event, some nine hundred thousand requests poured in for the available three hundred thousand tickets. The race sold out in just over a day.

The fans were not the only ones excited about the new race. NASCAR and Indy car drivers alike were eager for a chance to compete in and win the new event. A NASCAR record eighty-five entries were submitted for the forty available spots in the inaugural race. Speaking about the race, three-time NASCAR Winston Cup champion Darrell Waltrip said, "This is a big deal. Of all the deals I've been involved in, this is a big deal. We won't know how big a deal it was until we've gone down the road a ways, but this deal is big."[1]

Talking about the Indianapolis Motor Speedway and the new race, seven-time Winston Cup champion Dale Earnhardt said, "You get butterflies in your stomach and chill bumps when you walk out on pit road and look up at the racetrack. I'm proud to be a

FACT

The original surface of the Indianapolis Motor Speedway was made of crushed rock and tar. That surface broke up during the first races and was replaced with more than 3 million bricks before the first Indianapolis 500 in 1911. The original brick surface is what the speedway took the name brickyard from. The bricks were later paved over but remain under the track.

part of it, proud to be one of the first guys to be in the Brickyard 400—and hopefully will be proud to be the first guy to win it."[2]

Qualifying began the Thursday before the race. Midway through the day, thirty-seven-year-old NASCAR veteran Rick Mast set the speed to beat at 172.414 miles per hour.

Mast's lap held up, and he took the honor of starting the inaugural race on the pole. Beside him in the second starting spot was Dale Earnhardt. Jeff Gordon turned twenty-three on the first day of qualifying. He celebrated by capturing the third starting spot. Fifty-nine-year-old A. J. Foyt was a four-time Indianapolis 500 champion and winner of the 1972

The union between NASCAR racing and Indy car racing was announced on April 4, 1993. NASCAR and Indy car drivers alike were eager for a chance to compete in and win the new event. Cars coming into the first turn of the Indy 500 are shown here.

Daytona 500. He came out of retirement to qualify for the race and just made it. He would start in fortieth position. Two Indy car drivers, Danny Sullivan and Australia's Geoff Brabham, also qualified for the new race.

As race day dawned, every driver had one thing in mind. Each wanted to win the inaugural race and write his name in the history books. NASCAR veteran Ken Schrader echoed the popular sentiment of the day, "We can say this is just another race as far as winning the Winston Cup Championship, but that's just kidding yourself. I can't tell you who won the Indy 500 four years ago, but I can tell you Ray Harroun won the first one."[3]

With the call of "Gentlemen, start your engines," the race was under way. And as quickly as it began, there was trouble. Dale Earnhardt attempted to take the lead from Rick Mast on the first lap by going to the outside in turn four. He soon found out that the flat turns at the Indianapolis Motor Speedway can make passing tricky and dangerous. Coming out of the turn on the outside of Mast's car, Earnhardt lost control. His car slipped up the track and scraped the wall. Earnhardt quickly got his car under control and was able to keep racing. But the damage was done. He started drifting back in the field.

Luckily, on lap 3, there was a caution flag. This

The inaugural Brickyard 400 race turned into a difficult race to win for Dale Earnhardt (shown here). He lost control of his car coming out of a turn and had to struggle to catch up for the rest of the race.

allowed him to go into the pit to check the damage. Earnhardt's pit crew pulled the side of his car off the tire and sent him back out onto the track. But Earnhardt's scrape with the wall had hurt his chances of winning. He would continue to have trouble for the rest of the day. Said Earnhardt, "By the time we got our track position back [after the mishap], something else seemed to happen. We went to the front and to the back so many times today I lost count."[4]

Jeff Gordon, meanwhile, was feeling good. His car was strong. But Gordon had a close call of his own. On lap 66 of the 160-lap race, he was heading down pit road as Geoff Bodine was leaving his pit. Suddenly, the two cars were on a collision course. Said Gordon:

> I was getting ready to come in [to the pits] and Geoff was coming out, I knew he was going faster than me, . . . because he had on new tires. I waved my hand to let him know I was coming into the pits, but I don't know what he was thinking. He tried to go to the inside and that's where I was. It was very close. We actually rubbed, and it bent our left front fender. It could have been real bad, . . . but when it wasn't that's . . . when you know it's your day, that the guy upstairs is on your side.[5]

Gordon survived his scare and continued to race

with the leaders. For the first half of the race, Gordon battled the Bodine brothers, Geoff and Brett. But on lap 99, younger brother Brett gave Geoff a tap from behind. Geoff, who had taken the lead from his brother moments before, lost control of his car. As Geoff's car spun, he was hit by Dale Jarrett. The wreck knocked both drivers out of the race.

Following Geoff Bodine's early exit from the race, Gordon took control for a while. He clearly had one of the strongest cars on the track. But seasoned NASCAR veteran Ernie Irvan was moving up. Irvan had started the race in seventeenth position. He had found his groove and was running well. Indy driver Geoff Brabham was involved in an accident on lap 127. The resulting caution flag allowed Irvan to bunch up behind Gordon. Over the remaining laps, the race to win the inaugural Brickyard 400 would be between Gordon and Irvan.

Gordon and Irvan exchanged the lead five times over the final thirty laps. Both drivers were racing as hard as they could. Each took turns pushing the other. Irvan began the action by driving his Ford right up behind Gordon's bumper. This move disrupted the airflow around Gordon's car. The change in airflow causes the driver in front to lose some control of his car. As the cars roared through the turns at the Indianapolis Motor Speedway, the lead car would slip with its rear sliding toward the wall. Each driver was trying to see whether the other would crack and make a mistake.

"It was a mind game," said Ernie Irvan of his duel with Gordon. "When Jeff was in front of me, I could get him loose, so I just kept messing with him."[6] Said Gordon:

> Me and Ernie, we had one heck of a race going. The last guy I wanted to be racing was Ernie. There isn't anybody who can drive any harder than Ernie. I let him go around me, and then I did the same thing to him. I'd give it to him, he'd give it to me. I can't let him control my race. We were just counting down the laps because it wasn't doing me any good to be in front.[7]

It looked as if Gordon and Irvan would finish the race coming down the final straightaway side by side, battling for the victory. Gordon followed Irvan out of turn two with four laps to go. Then Irvan's car shook as his right front tire exploded. Gordon zoomed around Irvan's damaged car and into the lead. Irvan let off the accelerator as his car limped down the back straightaway.

Gordon took the checkered flag signaling victory. He was a comfortable ten car lengths ahead of second-place finisher Brett Bodine. Because of his misfortune, Irvan finished seventeenth. For the win,

FACT

On August 20, 1994, Ernie Irvan crashed head-on into the wall at the Michigan International Speedway at 200 miles per hour. He was given a 10 percent chance of survival. Among his injuries were a fractured skull, swollen brain, and collapsed lungs. Miraculously, however, Ernie Irvan recovered and began racing again fourteen months later. In June 1997, Irvan won the Miller 400 at the same speedway where he nearly died.

Gordon received a NASCAR record $613,000. This amount was more than twice that of the previous record payday for a Winston Cup victory.

Said Gordon:

> To me, this is the Indy 500 for stock car racing. When I went to NASCAR [from open-wheeled racing], I pretty much felt like my shot at driving at Indianapolis was gone. I thought I'd kissed it good-bye. Then to come here in a stock car and win, it's the greatest thing that's ever happened to me. I had to take an extra lap to let my emotions go, I was yelling so loud over the radio.[8]

The youngest driver in the race, Gordon had done it. By winning the prestigious Brickyard 400, he showed everyone that his victory earlier that year in the Coca-Cola 600 was no accident. It was obvious that Gordon, the 1993 Rookie of the Year, was learning what it took to compete and win at the highest level.

Gordon did not win any other races in 1994. Still, he cracked the top ten for the Winston Cup season standings with an impressive eighth-place finish. Heading into his third Winston Cup season, Jeff Gordon would be a driver to watch out for.

Chapter 7

Refuse to Lose

Before the 1995 season, the DuPont Automotive Finishes racing team came up with a motto for the year. It was, "Refuse to Lose." This was the attitude that the team wanted to carry through the thirty-one races on the 1995 Winston Cup circuit. The team had T-shirts made up with the motto. Said Gordon, "That's our motto this year. We're going to wear them every race this year. It's the attitude we want to take."[1]

Gordon began his third season with a twenty-second-place finish in the Daytona 500. But he would not be kept out of victory lane for long. With his "Refuse to Lose" attitude, Gordon headed into the Goodwrench 500 at the North Carolina Motor Speedway. It was the second race of the year, and

Gordon was eager to show everyone that his success in 1994 was real.

Gordon showed his determination and skill by capturing the pole. Then, on race day, Gordon out-raced Bobby Labonte and Dale Earnhardt for his first victory of the season.

After his first victory of the year, Gordon was asked whether he was thinking about the Winston Cup Championship. He responded, "You can't win one race and say we are going after the championship. But if we keep running like we have the first two races and stay consistent, we might find ourselves in the hunt."[2]

Gordon finished a dismal thirty-sixth in the third race of the season. He rebounded by winning the Purolator 500 in Atlanta. But he did not simply win this race; he dominated it. He led in 250 of the final 268 laps. As in his first victory of the season, Bobby Labonte finished second. Gordon and his DuPont teammates were making good on their "Refuse to Lose" slogan.

After the race in Atlanta, the Winston Cup series traveled to South Carolina for the Transouth 400. It would be at the dangerous Darlington Raceway. Gordon won the pole for the race. It was his third pole of the young season. The race was a different story, however. Gordon started out strong. Of the first 189 laps, Gordon led 155. Then, Bobby Labonte and rookie Randy LaJoie crashed on turn one. The resulting accident was right in Gordon's path. His car slammed head on into LaJoie's. The wreck knocked Gordon out of the race. He finished thirty-second.

Following his early exit at Darlington, Gordon traveled to the Bristol International Speedway in Tennessee. Bristol was not Gordon's favorite track. Every time he had raced at Bristol in the past, he had wrecked. This time, though, there would be no mishap. Gordon started the race second and ran well all day. He took control of the 342-lap race when he passed Mark Martin with ninety-nine laps to go. The race was not close. Gordon won by a remarkable 5.74 seconds over runner-up Rusty Wallace. It was his first victory on a short track. "This is awesome," Gordon said after the race. "Our only goal today was to come out with the car in one piece. We did that and a whole lot more."[3]

After the first five races of the season, Gordon led the circuit with three wins. He was fourth in the Winston Cup standings. Seven-time Winston Cup champion Dale Earnhardt was in first. Earnhardt and Richard Petty had both won seven Winston Cup titles. No driver had ever won eight. Earnhardt wanted to be the first. But with twenty-six races to

FACT

The Winston Cup Series races on three types of tracks. Superspeedways are at least one mile in length. The most well known superspeedways are Daytona, Talladega, and Charlotte. Short tracks are less than a mile in length. Famous short tracks include Bristol and Richmond. Road courses are narrow winding tracks with many turns. The two road courses in Winston Cup are Sears Point and Watkins Glen.

go, anything could happen. Even twenty-three year-old Jeff Gordon, racing in only his third Winston Cup season, had a chance.

Gordon raced well as the season continued, but he could not quite make it to victory lane. Over the next four races, he finished second twice and third twice. As the drivers headed back to the Daytona International Speedway for the Pepsi 400 in July, eight races had been run since his last win. Maybe Gordon's "Refuse to Lose" attitude was fading.

Richard Petty (whose number 43 car is shown here) was a seven-time Winston Cup Champion along with Dale Earnhardt.

For most of the Pepsi 400, Gordon battled Sterling Marlin for the lead. Then, with thirteen laps to go, Gordon had the lead to himself. But Earnhardt showed up in his rearview mirror. Gordon was

leading when an accident occurred with three laps to go. The accident brought out the yellow caution flag. The caution lasted for two laps. When the race restarted, there would be only one lap to go.

As Gordon prepared for the restart at Daytona, he would be ready. Driving down the front straightaway and heading for the start/finish line, Gordon slowed down. Slowing down would prevent the drivers behind him from having enough momentum to pass. When the green flag appeared, he slammed on the gas and took off. He left Earnhardt and the others in his dust. Gordon took the checkered flag for his first win in three months. On winning at Daytona, Gordon said, "This isn't the Daytona 500, but it's still Daytona."[4]

The win left Gordon seven points behind leader Sterling Marlin in the Winston Cup standings. Lurking in third, close behind Gordon, was Earnhardt. Gordon did not wait long to take the lead from Marlin. The week after his win at Daytona, Gordon won the Slick 50 300 at the New Hampshire International Speedway. He won despite wrecking his best car during his first qualifying run. The next day, Gordon qualified twenty-first in his backup car. On race day, Jeff Gordon drove his backup car to victory. The win moved him into first place in the standings for the season.

FACT

NASCAR driver Dale Earnhardt is nicknamed "The Intimidator" for his aggressive racing style. He dominated the Winston Cup Series from 1985 to 1994. During that ten year period, Earnhardt won 52 races and 6 Winston Cup Championships. For his career, Earnhardt is sixth in career wins (71) and tied for first in Winston Cup titles (7).

The 1995 season had its ups and downs for Jeff Gordon, but he took them all in stride.

Gordon had a second-place finish in the Miller Genuine Draft 500 at Pocono. Then he and the rest of the Winston Cup went to the Talladega Superspeedway in Alabama for the DieHard 500.

At Talladega, Gordon was having a good day. He started third and led the race for 97 of the first 126 laps, but disaster wasn't far off.

During the first of only two caution flags during the race, Gordon decided not to stop. He would not put new tires on the car. He decided not to pit because most of the other drivers had changed tires just a few laps earlier. He did not think that they would go into the pits again. If Gordon stopped to change his tires, he would lose the lead in the race. Instead, he decided to wait for the next caution flag to come into the pit. As the race wore on, however, no caution flags came out. Gordon's tires were wearing out and beginning to lose their grip on the track. By lap 139, Gordon was driving carefully on worn tires. He had fallen to seventh.

Coming around the second turn on lap 139, Gordon came up on the number 25 car, driven by his Hendrick Motorsports teammate Kenny Schrader. Gordon did not want to try to pass on the turn with worn tires. So, he got in line behind Schrader. As he slowed, the car driven by Ricky Craven came up behind him. The momentum from Craven's car gave

Gordon a push he did not need. Gordon had to make a choice.

> He [Ricky Craven] had a lot of momentum coming up on me, and that gave me a lot of momentum, so I was either going to run into the back of Kenny, or dive down to the low side or ride on the bottom until I could get back in line.[5]

Gordon drove his car down below Schrader's on the inside as they completed the second turn. As he did, his tires slipped and the front end of his car bumped into Schrader's car. Schrader lost control. After being bumped by Gordon, Schrader's car swerved, turned over, and flipped five times. Besides Schrader, the accident knocked out twelve other cars. One of them was Gordon's other teammate, Terry Labonte. Schrader luckily avoided any serious injury. He climbed out of his car with only a badly bruised right eye. Before the race was over, Kenny Schrader was on the cockpit radio trying to settle Gordon down.

Said Gordon,

> I've never met anybody like that Schrader. Most guys you put in the wall are waiting to punch you out, but before the race was over, he was on my radio assuring me that he wasn't upset with me. Obviously, inside, you know he was. As soon as I got home, I called to assure him I was concerned for him.[6]

Gordon remained in the race but failed to drive with his "Refuse to Lose" attitude.

> It was tough to keep going. I've never felt so bad after getting into somebody. You never want to see an accident like that, and you certainly don't want to be part of it. After that, every time somebody got beside me I was afraid that they were going to get sideways.[7]

Gordon finished eighth and remained in first place in the Winston Cup standings, but he was left shaken and upset. After the incident at Talladega, nobody knew how Gordon would respond. Would he continue to drive wide open? Or would he become conservative?

It did not take long to answer these questions. Gordon captured his eighth pole of the season for the next race. It was the second annual running of the Brickyard 400 at the Indianapolis Motor Speedway. On race day, unfortunately, Gordon was unable to defend his 1994 Brickyard 400 victory. He finished sixth. The day belonged to NASCAR superstar Dale Earnhardt. He beat Rusty Wallace for the win. The victory moved Earnhardt, third in the Winston Cup standings, closer to Gordon. Sterling Marlin remained second. With twelve races to go, the championship remained in Gordon's control.

Gordon continued to lead the race, bound for the

championship as the drivers headed back to Darlington for the Mountain Dew Southern 500. Earlier in the season, Gordon had crashed at Darlington while racing in the Transouth 400. This time he was planning on things being different. But once again, he found trouble. Gordon was racing in second on lap 137 of the 367-lap race when his car began to slide up the high-banked raceway. Gordon's car spun, but he managed to avoid hitting the wall and came sliding back down the racetrack. When he regained control of his car, Gordon had completed a 360-degree spin and was facing the right way.

His spin brought out the caution flag. Gordon hurried into the pits so that the Rainbow Warriors could make adjustments to his car. When he drove back on the track, he was in thirteenth place. Gordon spent the next 200 laps working his way back to the front. Then, with thirty-four laps to go, he passed Dale Earnhardt to take the lead.

As the race wore down, Gordon held on to the lead. With only a few laps to go, Gordon's crew chief Ray Evernham signaled him to come into the pits for four new tires. Gordon was looking to see what the cars behind him were going to do. He noticed that the second- and third-place cars were staying on the track. Gordon was heading down the entrance to pit road when he suddenly veered back onto the track to keep the lead. The move preserved the lead for Gordon, who went on to win. After the race, Evernham said, "What really won us the race is him watching Dale and Rusty in the mirror. I called him down pit road. That was a mistake. He watched his mirror, they didn't come, he stayed out and that won us the race."[8]

Two weeks later, Gordon won his seventh and final race of the season, the MBNA 500 at Dover Downs International Speedway in Delaware. This time, Gordon did not just dominate the field, he blew the other cars away. He led 400 of the 500 laps in the race, including the final 198.

Gordon went on to finish seventh and third in the next two races, before finishing a distant thirtieth at Charlotte in the twenty-eighth race of the season. His thirtieth-place finish broke a remarkable streak of fourteen top-ten finishes dating back to the middle of June. During that streak, Gordon took control of the race for the Winston Cup Championship. With three races left, the championship was in his grasp.

Going into the final race of the season, the NAPA 500 in Atlanta, all he had to do to win the championship was not finish last. And if he did finish last, Dale Earnhardt, who was in second place, would have to lead the most laps and win the race to take the title.

Jeff Gordon lived up to his "Refuse to Lose" motto during the 1995 racing season.

Gordon qualified eighth for the final event and raced cautiously, finishing thirty-second. He had done it. Jeff Gordon, just twenty-four years old, was the Winston Cup champion. Earnhardt, shooting for a record-breaking eighth Winston Cup title, finished second.

Gordon had lived up to his "Refuse to Lose" motto. In the process of winning the Winston Cup Championship, he won the most races (seven) and most poles (eight) for the season. Gordon also became the first driver to win more than $4 million in a season.

On winning his first Winston Cup, Gordon said:

> I know there's not a greater accomplishment for me than winning a NASCAR Winston Cup Championship, especially having the season we've had and having the career I've had. It's number one on my list right now. I really tried not to think about winning the championship before it happened, but I was prepared to enjoy it the next day.[9]

Chapter 8

Defending Champion

For defending Winston Cup champion Jeff Gordon, the 1996 season was filled with highs and lows. He won ten races, the most by any driver for the season. Despite that, however, he finished thirty-first or worse six times.

Unlike the previous four seasons, Gordon did not start the year off well. At the Daytona 500, Gordon crashed into the wall after only thirteen laps. He was knocked out of the race. He finished second to last. The next week at the North Carolina Motor Speedway, engine trouble caused Gordon to quit the race after only 134 of the 393 laps. As he had the previous week, he ended the race in second-to-last place. "This sport can humble you real quick," Gordon said after the race. "You think you're on top of the world—and the next thing you know, you're spun around backward."[1]

After the first two races of the season, Gordon was in forty-third place in the standings for the Winston Cup Championship. If he was going to defend his title, he had to turn things around fast.

The DuPont Automotive Finishes team regrouped quickly. Gordon qualified second for the next race in Richmond, Virginia. On race day, Gordon drove to his first win of the year. The victory was a team effort. Following 266 laps of racing without a caution period, Gordon was in fourth place with worn tires. He and crew chief Ray Evernham hoped for a caution flag. Gordon needed to bring his car into the

The DuPont Automotive Finishes team is known for its ability to work well together. The pit crew is shown here pushing Jeff Gordon's car. Gordon can be seen in front on the driver's side.

pit for new tires and gas. They got their wish on lap 350 when Darrell Waltrip hit the wall.

Gordon drove into the pit, and the Rainbow Warriors went to work. When they finished, Gordon raced back onto the track in first place on "special" tires. Evernham had adjusted the air pressure in the new tires. The car would handle better for short bursts of racing. He anticipated more caution flags over the remaining forty-nine laps. Evernham was right. There were four more caution periods before the race ended. After each caution, Gordon, racing on his special tires, drove his DuPont Chevrolet away from the competition. After his speedy pit crew put him in front on lap 351, he never lost the lead. Gordon won easily. "I needed this, the team needed this," Gordon said after the race. "We were real interested in not falling completely on our faces. It has been difficult going through the trouble we had the first two races."[2]

Gordon finished third in the next race of the season, the Purolator 500 in Atlanta. Then he outdueled Dale Jarrett to win the Transouth 400 at Darlington. Gordon led Jarrett as the 293-lap event was winding down. Jarrett was driving hard to catch up. On lap 279, Gordon got caught behind a slower car. This allowed Jarrett to pass and take the lead. Gordon was now chasing Jarrett, but Evernham told him not to worry. He had calculated that Jarrett could not finish without stopping for fuel.

Gordon raced in second and waited. With seven laps to go, however, Jarrett attempted to pass the lapped car of Dave Marcis on the outside of turn four. As he did, Marcis drifted up the track and pinched Jarrett's car between his car and the wall. The incident damaged Jarrett's car enough to allow Gordon to pass easily. Two laps later, he took the checkered flag for his second win of the year. Jarrett ran out of gas on the last lap and finished fifteenth.

The win moved Gordon, the defending Winston Cup champion, into ninth place in the Winston Cup standings. It was the first time Gordon had cracked the top ten all season. He had come a long way since his first two disastrous starts of the year.

The next week, Gordon captured his third victory by winning the rain-shortened Food City 500. He finished second and third in the races that followed. Since his engine failure in the second race of the season, Gordon had put together a streak of six top-five finishes. This moved him all the way up to second in the season standings behind Dale Earnhardt. Then, once again, trouble visited Gordon. He got caught in a fourteen-car pileup in the Winston Select 500 at the Talladega Superspeedway in Alabama. He finished a disappointing thirty-third.

Gordon's fourth win of the year came in the twelfth race of the season at Dover Downs International Speedway in Delaware. At Dover, Gordon led the final 128 laps of the 500-lap race. He easily beat the second-place car, driven by his Hendrick Motorsports teammate Terry Labonte. After Dover, the Winston Cup series headed to the Pocono Raceway in Pennsylvania for the UAW-GM Teamwork 500. This was the same track where a blown shift in 1995 cost him a win.

Gordon won the pole for the race, his third pole of the season and third in a row. Then he prepared to make up for his error the previous year. As in the previous race at Dover, Gordon ran well and kept his DuPont Chevrolet up front. He led 94 of the 200 laps, including the final 29 as he cruised to victory. "I hadn't forgotten what happened last year," Gordon said after the race. "I was scared every time I shifted today during the last 20 laps."[3]

Gordon finished sixth and third in the fourteenth and fifteenth races of the year. But in the sixteenth race at the New Hampshire International Speedway, Gordon's up-and-down season went south again. An engine problem caused him to drop out of the race. He finished thirty-fourth.

Gordon clung to third in the Winston Cup standings when he traveled back to Talladega for the

DieHard 500. At Talladega, rain delayed the start of the race for nearly four hours. The race was further delayed by a pair of accidents that affected more than half the cars in the race. The second accident took out Gordon's main competitor, Dale Earnhardt.

When the race restarted, the remaining drivers were notified that the race was being shortened from 188 laps to 129 because of darkness. The race would end in five laps.

The accident had knocked out the cars that were running one and two. It slowed the third-place car driven by Ernie Irvan. Gordon was in fourth before the accident. He was in first for the restart. "How did I get by?" Gordon said about the big wreck. "I went as far left as I could and stood on the gas to get by it as fast as I could."[4]

At the restart, Gordon hit the gas pedal and held on. He drove hard and was able to hold off the cars behind him for the win, his sixth of the year. The win moved Gordon into first place in the Winston Cup standings for the first time of the season.

His lead did not last long, however. Gordon wrecked in the next race, the Brickyard 400 at the Indianapolis Motor Speedway. He finished a disappointing thirty-seventh. The poor finish dropped him to fourth in the Winston Cup standings.

Gordon had moved back up to second in the

The DieHard 500 in 1996 proved difficult for Jeff Gordon's fellow racers as an accident knocked out the car driven by Dale Earnhardt and slowed the third-place car driven by Ernie Irvan (shown here with his daughter at Daytona).

Winston Cup standings. As he prepared for the Southern 500 at Darlington on September 1, Terry Labonte was in first.

At the Southern 500, all eyes were on Dale Jarrett. Jarrett had won two of NASCAR's four big races. He would collect the Winston Million bonus if he could win this race. Jarrett found out quickly that this wasn't going to be his day. On lap 46 of the 367-lap race, Jarrett hit an oil slick on the track and slid into the wall. He did not collect the Winston Million that day.

Gordon, meanwhile, was struggling with handling problems. That turned out to be lucky. "I was running maybe seventh or eighth or something like that when the wreck with the leaders happened early in the race," Gordon said. "I went high of the oil on the track and had checked up, so I didn't go through it at full speed like the leaders did. That saved us. Had I been up front, I would have been wrecked."[5]

The next leader of the race, Jimmy Spencer, spun out on lap 166 and lost a lap. After Spencer's trouble, Hut Stricklin took over the race. Gordon battled Stricklin for a while, but Stricklin's car appeared to be better, and he began to pull away. Just as it looked like Stricklin would cruise to an easy win, his car began to overheat. As the problem got worse, Gordon

FACT

Since 1985, any driver who has won three of the four major Winston Cup races (Daytona 500, Winston 500, Coca-Cola 600, Southern 500), has collected $1 million—the Winston Million. Bill Elliott collected the Winston Million in 1985. From 1986 to 1997, four drivers began the Southern 500 with a shot at the $1 million. Jeff Gordon was the only one who collected the Winston Million.

closed in for the kill. With fifteen laps to go, Gordon caught and passed Stricklin's ailing car. Gordon kept on going and won the race by more than five seconds over Stricklin. The win was Gordon's seventh of the year, matching the total from his 1995 championship season.

FACT

NASCAR awards points to each driver in each Winston Cup race on a sliding scale. The winner gets 175 points. Each driver to follow receives a specific number of points less than the driver ahead of him. Each driver to lead the race gets five additional points. Whoever leads the most laps gets five more points. The driver with the most points at the end of the season wins the Winston Cup Championship.

At Richmond the following week, Gordon finished second, less than a car length behind winner Ernie Irvan. Then he headed back to Dover where he had won the last two Winston Cup races. Once again, Gordon dominated the field at Dover. He held off a hard-charging Rusty Wallace over the last fifty laps. Gordon won for the third consecutive time at Dover. It was his eighth win of the year and it moved him back into first place in the Winston Cup standings.

Gordon's season was hitting another high note. After Dover, he went to the Martinsville Speedway in Virginia. He edged out Terry Labonte for his ninth win of the year. Next, the Winston Cup series headed to the North Wilkesboro Speedway in North Carolina. Gordon held off Dale Earnhardt for his third win in a row. It was his tenth win of the year, and it increased his chances for a second Winston Cup Championship.

Gordon's good fortune, however, would not last in his yo-yo season. Racing in first the following week at the Charlotte Motor Speedway, his engine began to overheat. Quickly, Gordon headed into the pit to see about the problem. The car had a cracked cylinder. The DuPont team managed to keep the engine going, but Gordon knew that it would be a rough day. He finished thirty-first, fifteen laps behind winner Terry Labonte. Terry Labonte, his teammate, was in second place in the Winston Cup standings for the year. The win, coupled with Gordon's trouble, moved Labonte to one point behind Gordon for the title.

At the next race, Gordon finished twelfth. Terry Labonte crossed the finish line in third, to take the Winston Cup lead away from Gordon. The following week at Phoenix, Labonte finished third. He beat Gordon again, who finished fifth. With one race to go, Gordon was in second place in the Winston Cup standings. He trailed teammate Terry Labonte. Gordon's luck had to change if he was going to defend his Winston Cup title.

"You never know when you're going to win six or seven races in a row when things are going great, and you've got to enjoy that while you can and not think about when the bad ones are going to come," Gordon said during his late-season slump. "When they do happen, you can't get down. You've got to keep your head up and go to the next race."[6]

Gordon knew that he would have to run well in the final race to win his second Winston Cup Championship. Prior to the final race, Gordon said, "There's not a very big margin between us, so we've got to go all out and those guys are going to have to protect their lead. It'll be interesting. Anything can happen."[7]

Unfortunately, Gordon had trouble again. A problem with one of his rear tires caused him to head to the pits early in the race. When he reentered the race, he was two laps down. Gordon raced hard. He managed to make up the two laps and even briefly battled for the lead before finishing third.

It did not matter. Terry Labonte continued the strong, consistent racing he had done all year and finished fifth. It was his twenty-first top-five finish of the year. Despite winning only two races all season, Terry Labonte was the 1996 Winston Cup champion. Gordon finished second. "We knew if Terry didn't have a problem, we didn't have a chance," said Gordon after the race. "We at least wanted to make him work for it, and we did."[8]

It was Labonte's second Winston Cup Championship. He had captured the title twelve years earlier, in 1984. After finishing second for the Winston Cup Championship, Gordon said, "We know how a championship is won—we proved that last year. We're happy we won ten races. But I'd trade places with Terry in a second."[9] Gordon was not planning on putting that much time between his first and second Winston Cup titles. His "Refuse to Lose" attitude would propel him toward yet another season—and another opportunity to win.

Chapter 9

Six Million-Dollar Man

During the winter before the 1997 season, Jeff Gordon received terrible news. Rick Hendrick, his team owner and friend, was diagnosed with leukemia, a life-threatening form of cancer. Hendrick's illness would prevent him from attending any races in 1997.

The night before the Daytona 500, Gordon called his ailing boss. "I'm going to make you smile tomorrow," he promised. "I'll have you high-fiving everybody in your house."[1] To keep his promise, Gordon had to overcome a problem with one of his tires midway through the race. He outraced Dale Earnhardt and Bill Elliott for his first Daytona 500 victory. His Hendrick Motorsports teammates, Terry Labonte and Ricky Craven, finished second and third. The team had completed an unprecedented sweep in NASCAR's biggest race. The three drivers dedicated the race to their ailing boss.

In victory lane, Gordon spoke with Hendrick on a mobile phone. Hendrick called the win the "best medicine" he could get. Gordon dedicated the rest of the season to his sick friend.

A week after his dramatic win at Daytona, Gordon overtook Dale Jarrett with forty-three laps to go to win the Goodwrench 400. Jarrett led 323 of the first 350 laps in the 393-lap race. Then Gordon passed him. "You've got to give Jeff and his guys credit," Jarrett said. "We didn't slow down. Jeff picked his pace up."[2] With the victory, Gordon became the first driver since David Pearson in 1976 to win the first two races of the year. Gordon, the 1996 runner-up, was in first place in the Winston Cup standings. He stayed in the top five all season.

Gordon had slipped to fifth place in the season standings when the Winston Cup series headed to the Bristol Motor Speedway in Tennessee. At Bristol, Gordon bumped by Rusty Wallace on the final lap for the win.

"The fans seated in turn three stands had a real show to watch," Gordon said afterward. "I was able to get the run off turn two. Rusty got sideways a little, then I touched him. I look at that as being typical

FACT

Leukemia is a kind of cancer caused by abnormal white blood cells growing in an uncontrolled way. These abnormal cells interfere with the production of normal white blood cells which fight infection. Symptoms of leukemia include fatigue, paleness, weight loss, repeated infections, also bruising easily, and nosebleeds. Although leukemia is the number one disease killer of children, ten times as many adults are diagnosed with it.

racing."[3] Wallace agreed: "He might have touched me a little, but I'd have done the same thing going for the win."[4]

Following this victory at Bristol, Gordon won the Goody's 500 at the Martinsville Speedway in Virginia. Gordon led an incredible 431 out of 500 laps and survived a scare. On lap 327, Gordon collided with Jimmy Spencer in turn four. The collision caused both cars to spin. Miraculously, both drivers spun in a complete circle and continued racing down the track. The incident briefly cost Gordon the lead. He regained it for good on lap 376 when he passed Bobby Hamilton. With wins at Bristol and

During the winter before the 1997 season, team owner Rick Hendrick was diagnosed with leukemia, a life-threatening form of cancer. Jeff Gordon (in the middle holding up sign) dedicated the Daytona 500 to his friend.

Martinsville, Gordon moved up to third in the battle for the Winston Cup Championship.

Gordon finished fifth in the next race, the Winston 500. It was the second of the four races that make up the Winston Million. He had already won the first of the four races, the Daytona 500. The following week, Gordon won the pole for the Coca-Cola 600, the third race in the Winston Million. An accident during his first pit stop on lap 53, however, put him at the back of the pack. In the pit, a tire removed from Gordon's car bumped into the jack, causing the car to crash down, damaging the right front end. By the time the damage was repaired, he had dropped to thirty-eighth.

Gordon raced hard through the pack of cars for the next 142 laps. He made it to third before rain caused the race to be stopped for two and a half hours. The race is run at night under the lights at the Charlotte Motor Speedway in North Carolina. It had already been rain delayed for a half hour at the start. By 12:45 A.M., NASCAR officials were concerned about the late time. They gave the signal to all drivers that there were twenty laps to go. The race was being shortened to 333 laps instead of the usual 400. When the signal came, Gordon was in second, trailing Rusty Wallace. He passed Wallace three laps later and pulled away for the victory.

Gordon had captured two of the four races that make up the Winston Million. If he could win the Southern 500 at the end of August, he would become only the second driver to collect the Winston Million.

Two weeks later, racing in the Pocono 500, Gordon overcame a cut tire twenty laps into the race to win. It was Gordon's sixth win of the year, moving him into a first-place tie with teammate Terry Labonte in the Winston Cup standings.

Gordon had first place to himself when the Winston Cup series moved to the brand-new California Speedway for the California 500. The California 500 came down to a game of strategy and fuel conservation. With forty-seven laps to go, Gordon was in the lead with Mark Martin close behind. Crew chief Ray Evernham calculated that Martin could not make it to the finish without stopping for gas. He also calculated that Gordon would run out of gas one lap short of the finish. Evernham radioed Gordon and told him to conserve gas.

In an attempt to conserve gas, Gordon slowed and let Martin pass with sixteen laps to go. Gordon was racing in Martin's draft, allowing him to break the wind. This maneuver allows the driver in the draft to let off the accelerator slightly, thus saving gas. Martin held the lead until pitting with ten laps to go. At that point, Gordon took the lead again. To keep the lead and continue to conserve gas, Gordon raced hard into the turns and then eased off the accelerator, allowing momentum to pull his car through. The strategy worked. Gordon held off teammate Terry Labonte for the win. He ran out of gas just as he crossed the finish line. "I learned how to conserve fuel today," Gordon said after the win. "I never had to do that before. It was interesting."[5]

Gordon was unable to reach victory lane during the next four races. Then the Winston Cup Series went to Watkins Glen, New York, for the Bud at the Glen road race. In his Winston Cup career, Gordon had never won a road race.

At Watkins Glen, Gordon was in front with twenty-five laps to go when Rusty Wallace attempted to pass on a restart. Not wanting to lose the lead, he cut Wallace off and sent him off the course as the green flag waved, signaling the restart. Gordon went on to win. It was his eighth victory of the season and his first-ever road course win.

Asked about the incident with Wallace after the race, Gordon said, "That's what happens when you jump the start—you're going to get pushed out of there."[6] Wallace, who got edged out by Gordon earlier in the year at Bristol, had no complaints.

Gordon led the Winston Cup standings after his

win in the Bud at the Glen. But by the time he went to the Darlington Raceway in South Carolina for the Southern 500, he had slipped into second. If Gordon could win the Southern 500, he would collect the Winston Million.

For most of the race, Gordon battled handling problems. During every pit stop, the Rainbow Warriors made adjustments to set the car right. Gordon was able to hang on despite his troubles. Then, as the race wound down, everything began to come together. With eight laps to go, Gordon had the lead with Dale Jarrett and Jeff Burton close behind. Burton passed Jarrett to move into second with three laps to go. When the white flag flew, it was Burton who was trying to take the race and the Winston Million away from Gordon.

Racing out of turn four and down the front straightaway heading into the final lap, Burton attempted to take the lead by pulling inside of Gordon. Gordon, however, was not about to let Burton get by. "When we came off four, I shot straight down, and I don't think he was expecting that," Gordon said. "He actually lifted the back of my car off the ground, and I was just happy I kept going straight. I thought I was going to spin."[7] The cars continued to rub together as the two drivers raced through turns one and two, Burton trying to get by and Gordon fighting him off. Gordon, however, successfully blocked Burton's attempts to pass and pulled away to win. It was his third Southern 500 win in as many years.

By winning the Daytona 500, Coca-Cola 600, and Southern 500 in the same year, Jeff Gordon became only the second driver to collect the Winston Million. "This is just unbelievable," he said. "I never thought anyone would win the one million again, let alone three straight Southern 500s."[8]

Two weeks later, Gordon won his tenth and final race of the season when he captured the CMT 300 at the New Hampshire International Speedway. Racing on worn tires, Gordon skillfully held off Ernie Irvan over the final seventy-two laps to win by a car length. The victory left Gordon in first place for the Winston Cup Championship, 139 points ahead of Mark Martin.

Gordon continued to lead the battle for the Winston Cup as the season neared the finish, but trouble at Talladega in October threatened his hold. At Talladega for the DieHard 500, Gordon's left front tire blew while he was at the front of a large pack of cars. After the tire went, he slammed into John Andretti's car and then into the wall. In the resulting accident, twenty-three cars were banged up, including the top five in the Winston Cup

FACT

Jeff Gordon won 29 races in his first five Winston Cup seasons (1993–1997). In comparison, here are the number of wins other drivers had in their first five seasons: Richard Petty, 27; Darrell Waltrip, 22; Rusty Wallace, 10; Dale Earnhardt, 9; Mark Martin, 5; Terry Labonte, 2; Dale Jarrett, 1.

standings. Gordon walked away from the wreck, but his day was over. He finished thirty-fifth. His lead in Winston Cup standings was shrinking.

Gordon saw his lead shrink to seventy-seven points going into the final race of the season in Atlanta. Dale Jarrett had caught Mark Martin and was in second. Martin was ten points behind Jarrett in third. At Atlanta for the NAPA 500, Gordon could clinch his second Winston Cup Championship by finishing eighteenth or better.

It was not going to be easy. While warming up his tires as he eased down pit road before his qualifying lap, Gordon lost control of his car and slammed into Bobby Hamilton's parked Pontiac. Gordon damaged the front of his car so severely that the Rainbow Warriors had to scramble to get his backup car ready to qualify. Gordon took off on his qualifying lap in his backup car, which had not been tested on the track. His lap did not go well. He barely made the field. He would start the final race of the season thirty-seventh.

Gordon drove conservatively when the final race began. His goal was to finish fifteenth. Driving cautiously, he made it to tenth place with fifty-six laps to go when he pitted for new tires. When he left pit road he had slipped to nineteenth.

As the race neared the end, Gordon battled back

into seventeenth. If he could hold on, he would win the championship. The new surface on the Atlanta track, however, had wreaked havoc with tires all day. Gordon was not sure his tires would last to the finish. As the final laps passed, he grew concerned that a tire would go and cost him the title. "Even when they waved the white flag, I wasn't comfortable because I was afraid a tire could blow at any moment," said Gordon. "Only when I came off turn four on the last lap and knew that I could get to the line even if a tire went, did I sigh in relief."[9]

Gordon had won his second Winston Cup Championship. After the race, he spoke over the phone to his ailing team owner Rick Hendrick, who was at home in North Carolina. Both men congratulated each other. Hendrick declared the championship more "good medicine." On winning his second Winston Cup Championship, Gordon said, "Coming off last year, not winning the championship made us that hungrier. To win two championships is the sweetest thing ever."[10]

For the season, Gordon earned a Winston Cup record, $6,375,658, becoming NASCAR's first 6 million-dollar man. In the process, he shattered the $4,347,343 record for winnings in a season that he set in 1995.

In only five seasons of Winston Cup racing,

For the 1997 season, Jeff Gordon (shown here embracing his wife) earned a Winston Cup record $6,375,658 to become NASCAR's first 6 million-dollar man.

Gordon had won twenty-nine races and two Winston Cup Championships. DuPont crew chief Ray Evernham sums up Gordon well:

> There's something that separates some people from the rest. He's like Michael Jordan. There's something that makes Jeff Gordon different from other drivers. Every race I see change, and it's all been for the good. He does things every week that amaze me.[11]

If Gordon continues to win races at the pace he has since 1994, he will top Richard Petty's record (of 200 victories) in 2024. In a sport where the average age of the top drivers is almost forty and athletes can continue to race well into their fifties, no one seems more likely to take Petty's title as the "king" of stock car racing than Jeff Gordon.

Gordon continued to dominate the Winston Cup series in 1998. Between June and October of that year, he put together an amazing streak of 17 top-five finishes, including four wins in a row. During that span of races, Gordon also wrapped up his third Winston Cup title in four years. At just twenty-seven, Gordon was the youngest driver to win three Winston Cup championships.

For the fourth year in a row, Gordon also led the series with 13 wins. In addition, he became the first driver to twice win the prestigious Brickyard 400.

For his efforts in 1998, Gordon won $9,306,584, shattering the single-season record for winnings he had previously set in 1997.

Gordon also received good news on another front in 1998. Team owner Rick Hendrick, who continued to battle leukemia, saw his cancer go into near-complete remission. Although doctors did not give him a totally clean bill of health, they are hopeful that he will make a full recovery.

After his sixth season of Winston Cup racing and a win at the Daytona 500 in 1999, Jeff Gordon shows no signs of slowing down. As the youngest driver competing, Gordon seems likely to dominate NASCAR for many years to come.

Chapter Notes

Chapter 1. The Daytona 500

1. Jim McLaurin, "Gordon Avoids Mishaps, Wins Daytona," *1997 Cyberstate, The State* (Columbia, S.C.), February 17, 1997, <http://www.thestate.com>, February 17, 1997.

2. Gene Bryson, "Earnhardt, Can He Break the Jinx?" *Sunday News Journal* (Wilmington, Del.), February 16, 1997, p. 1E.

3. Raad Cawthon, "Gordon Is Roadblock in Earnhardt's Path to Victory," *The Philadelphia Inquirer*, February 16, 1997, p. C1.

4. Raad Cawthon, "Gordon Wins With Gutsy Moves at Daytona," *Philadelphia Online, The Philadelphia Inquirer*, February 17, 1997, <http://www.phillynews.com>, February 17, 1997.

5. Ed Hinton, "Safety in Numbers: Jeff Gordon and his Teammates Ganged Up on the Daytona 500 Field for an Unprecedented 1–2–3 Finish," *Sports Illustrated*, February 24, 1997, p. 33.

6. Ibid.

7. Curt Cavin, "Jeff Gordon Leads a 1-2-3 Team Hendrick Punch," *Speednet, The Indianapolis Star/News*, February 16, 1997, <http://speednet.starnews.com> February 17, 1997.

Chapter 2. NASCAR Racing Basics

No notes.

Chapter 3. Kid Racer

1. Ed Hinton, "On the Fast Track—At 23, Jeff Gordon is NASCAR's Hottest Driver and Biggest Hope for the Future," *Sports Illustrated,* August 24, 1995, p. 46.

2. Ibid.

3. Scott Fowler, "Jeff Gordon: Right On Track," *The Charlotte Observer*, May 28, 1995, p. A1.

4. Ed Hinton, "A Sudden Star," *Sports Illustrated Presents the NASCAR 1996 Winston Cup Series* (Special Collector's Edition), p. 50.

5. Fowler, p. A1.

6. Hinton, "On the Fast Track," p. 48.

7. Fowler, p. A1.

8. Pat Jordan, "Speed Racer," *TV Guide,* August 2–8, 1997, p. 22.

9. Hinton, "On the Fast Track," p. 48.

Chapter 4. Busch Grand National Racing

1. Jim McLaurin, "Gordon Arrives in Style," *The State* (Columbia, S.C.), March 15, 1992, p. C4.

2. Jim McLaurin, "A Star Is Born in Passing Lane to Top of NASCAR," *The State* (Columbia, S.C.), May 29, 1992, p. C1.

3. Ron Green, "A Big Day for Racing's Next Big Star," *The Charlotte Observer,* May 24, 1992, p. D1.

4. Tom Higgins, "Gordon Sweeps to Victory," *The Charlotte Observer*, October 11, 1992, p. C1.

5. Ibid.

6. Jim McLaurin, "Gordon Sets Record With 11th GN Pole," *The State* (Columbia, S.C.), October 23, 1992, p. C5.

7. Ed Hinton, "A Sudden Star," *Sports Illustrated Presents The NASCAR 1996 Winston Cup Series* (Special Collector's Edition), p. 50.

Chapter 5. Victory Lane

1. Pat Jordan, "Speed Racer," *TV Guide*, August 2–8, 1997, p. 22.

2. Stan Olson, "Gordon Gobbles Up Goals for Rookie Year," *The Charlotte Observer*, October 11, 1993, p. B4.

3. Steve Ballard, "Gordon Flashes Brilliance by Taking Pole," *USA Today*, May 27, 1994, p. 15.

4. Jim McLaurin, "Pole-Winner Gordon Credits Work By Crew," *The State* (Columbia, S.C.), May 26, 1994, p. C1.

5. Tom Higgins, "Gordon Picks Up Pieces, Wins Pole Rebuilt Car to Lead 600 On Sunday," *The Charlotte Observer*, May 26, 1994, p. 1B

6. Ballard, p. 15.

7. Don Coble, "Jeff Gordon Was Groomed to Be a Racer," *Gannett News Services*, May 30, 1994, <http://www.elibrary.com>, October 22, 1998.

8. Don Coble, "Jeff Gordon Was the Youngest," *Gannett News Services*, May 29, 1994, <http://www.elibrary.com>, October 22, 1998.

9. Liz Clarke, "Gordon's Victory Revolved Around Tire Strategy," *The Charlotte Observer*, May 30, 1994, p. B9.

10. Tom Higgins, "Young Gun Bags 600 Win; Gordon, 22, Cashes In On 2-Tire Gamble," *The Charlotte Observer*, May 30, 1994, p. B1.

Chapter 6. The Brickyard 400

1. Bruce Newman, "Taking Stock," *Sports Illustrated*, April 16, 1994, p. 26.

2. Beth Tuschak, "We're All Rookies Here," *USA Today*, August 5, 1994, p. C1.

3. Ibid.

4. Gary Long, "Gordon Brings Home History With Brickyard 400 Victory," *The Miami Herald*, August 7, 1994, p. C1.

5. Shav Glick, "Gordon Prevails in Brickyard 400," *The Los Angeles Times*, August 7, 1994, Sports, p. 1.

6. Newman, p. 25.

7. Sally Pollack, "Jeff Gordon Triumphs in Race of the Future," *The Philadelphia Inquirer*, August 7, 1994, p. C1.

8. Glick, pp. C1, C8.

Chapter 7. Refuse to Lose

1. Wire Service, "Gordon Dominates at Rockingham," *The San Jose Mercury News*, February 27, 1995, p. E2.

2. Monte Dutton, "Day by Day," *The 1995 Indianapolis Stock Cars Yearbook*, p. 24.

3. Associated Press, "At Long Last, Gordon Has Short-track Victory," *The Los Angeles Times*, April 3, 1995, Sports, p. 9.

4. Gary Long, "Wonder Boy Gordon Catches On in a Hurry," *The Miami Herald*, July 2,1995, Sports, p. D12.

5. Jim McLaurin, "Gordon Shaken, but Not Rattled: Points Leader Learns from DieHard Race," *The State* (Columbia, S.C.), July 28, 1995, p. C5.

6. Shav Glick, "A Veteran Champion at Only 24, Auto Racing: Gordon's Visage Belies His 19 Years of Driving Cars Fast—and Winning," *The Los Angeles Times*, August 3, 1995, Sports, p. C9.

7. Tom Higgins, "Schrader Took Wild Ride, but Gordon Left Shaken—Teammate Accepts Blame for 13-Car Pileup," *The Charlotte Observer*, July 24, 1995, p. B5.

8. Matt Dutton, "Wonderboy or Just a Kid?" *The 1995 Indianapolis Stock Cars Yearbook*, p. 204.

9. "Jeff Gordon, 1995 NASCAR Winston Cup Champion," *The 1996 Official Directory for the NASCAR Winston Cup Series*, p. 19.

Chapter 8. Defending Champion

1. Bruce Newman, "On Track Again," *Sports Illustrated Presents the NASCAR 1996 Winston Cup Series* (Special Collector's Edition), p. 34.

2. Tom Higgins, "Gordon Out of Pits, Into Victory Lane," *The Charlotte Observer,* March 4, 1996, <http://www.charlotte.com/observer>, October 23, 1998.

3. Tom Higgins, "Gordon's Shift of Fortune Means Victory at Pocono," *The Charlotte Observer,* June 17, 1996, <http://www.charlotte.com/observer>, October 23, 1998.

4. Tom Higgins, "Gordon Survives Wild Talladega," *The Charlotte Observer*, July 29, 1996, <http://www.newslibrary.infinet/char/>, October 23, 1998.

5. Ben White, "To Thine Own Self Be True," *NASCAR Winston Cup Illustrated* (Charlotte, N.C.: Street & Smith's Sport Group, November 1996), p. 77.

6. Mike Hembree, "Gordon Has Eye on Winston Cup Points Finish Line," *Gannett News Service,* October 17, 1996, <http://www.elibrary.com>, October 23, 1998.

7. Gene Bryson, "Low-Key Labonte Looks to Lock Up Winston Cup," *The News Journal*, November 8, 1996, p. C2.

8. Steve Ballard, "B. Labonte: Dream Finale 'Coolest Thing' in My Life," *USA Today*, November 11, 1996, p. C3.

9. Ed Hinton, "Brother Act," *Sports Illustrated Presents the NASCAR 1996 Winston Cup Series* (Special Collector's Edition), p. 138.

Chapter 9. Six Million-Dollar Man

1. Ed Hinton, "True to His Word," *Sports Illustrated Presents the NASCAR 1997 Winston Cup* (Special Collector's Edition), p. 25.

2. "Gordon Finds 'Groove,' Wins Goodwrench 400," *USA Today*, February 24, 1997, p. C5.

3. Bill Luther, "Late Break Gives Gordon His Third Food City 500 Win," *The Knoxville News–Sentinel Online*, April 1997, <http://www.knoxnews.com>, April 14, 1997.

4. Steve Ballard, "Daring Gordon Bags Food City 500 Title," *USA Today*, April 14, 1997, p. C11.

5. Mike Harris, Associated Press, "No Fueling Around in Gordon Win," *The News Journal* (Wilmington, Del.), June 23, 1997, p. C1.

6. Ed Hinton, "Road Warrior," *Sports Illustrated Presents the NASCAR 1997 Winston Cup* (Special Collector's Edition), p. 109.

7. Benny Phillips, "Jeff's Million-Dollar Southern 500," in *Stock Car Racing*, ed. William G. Holder (Greenwich, Conn.: Brampton, 1994), p. 72.

8. Steve Waid, "Gordon Rides Into History With Darlington Win," NASCAR Online—NASCAR Winston Cup Scene, August 31, 1997, <http://www.NASCAR.com>, August 31, 1997.

9. Ed Hinton, "It Wasn't Pretty, but Jeff Gordon and His Hendrick Motorsports Crew Narrowly Averted Disaster to Win Their Second Winston Cup," *Sports Illustrated*, November 24, 1997, p. 86.

10. The Associated Press, "Gordon 17th, and Champ," *The Philadelphia Daily News*, November 17, 1997, p. 90.

11. Don Coble, "Just One Start Away From a Virtual Sure-Thing NASCAR Winston Cup Championship, Jeff Gordon and Crew Chief Ray Evernham Haven't Veered Off Course," *Gannett News Services*, November 6, 1995, <http://www.elibrary.com>, October 22, 1998.

Career Statistics

Season	Races Started	Wins	Top 5s	Top 10s	Poles	Earnings	Winston Cup Standings
1992	1	0	0	0	0	6,285	N/A
1993	30	0	7	11	1	765,168	14
1994	31	2	7	14	1	1,779,523	8
1995	31	7	17	23	8	4,347,343	1
1996	31	10	21	24	5	3,428,485	2
1997	32	10	22	23	1	6,375,658	1
1998	33	13	26	28	7	9,306,584	1
Totals	189	42	100	123	23	26,009,046	3 Winston Cup Titles

Where to Write Jeff Gordon

On the Internet at:

Jeff Gordon's Official NASCAR site:
<http://www.jeffgordon.com>

Jeff Gordon National Fan Club:
<http://www.JeffGordonFanClub.com>

NASCAR Online:
<http://www.nascar.com>

Index

A

Atlanta Motor Speedway, 17, 29, 34, 68, 86–87

B

Bickford, John, 21
bicycle motocross racing (BMX), 22
black flag, 16
Bodine, Brett, 50, 51
Bodine, Geoff, 41, 43, 49, 50
Brickyard 400, 45, 50, 52, 61, 71, 89
Bristol Motor Speedway, 55, 79
Buck Baker NASCAR Driving School, 27
Bud at the Glen, 83
Bud Shootout, 18
Burton, Jeff, 8, 84–85
Busch Clash, 18, 39

C

California 500, 82
Charlotte Motor Speedway, 31, 41, 63, 75, 81
checkered flag, 16
Coca-Cola 600, 39, 52, 81, 85
Connerly, Hugh, 27
Craven, Ricky, 10–11, 13, 59, 78

D

Darlington Raceway, 54–55, 62, 68, 84
Davis, Bill, 28
Daytona 500, 7–9, 13, 17, 19, 35, 38–39, 53, 66, 78, 81, 85
Daytona International Speedway, 56–57
Dover Downs International Speedway, 63, 70, 74
draft, 14, 82
drafting, 14
DuPont, 34

E

Earnhardt, Dale, 9–10, 30, 40, 45–49, 54–57, 61–65, 69, 71, 74
Elliott, Bill, 9–11, 37, 78
Evernham, Ray, 7, 35, 41, 62–63, 67–68, 82, 89

F

Foyt, A. J., 46
France Jr., Bill, 45

G

go-kart, 23
Gordon, Brooke, 37–38
green flag, 15

H

Hamilton, Bobby, 80, 86
Hendrick, Rick, 34, 40, 78–79, 87, 90

I

Indianapolis 500, 44, 47
Indianapolis Motor Speedway, 25, 44–45, 50, 61, 71

Irvan, Ernie, 10, 50–51, 71, 74

J

Jarrett, Dale, 10, 29, 68–69, 73, 79, 84, 86

L

Labonte, Bobby, 54–55
Labonte, Terry, 10–11, 13, 60, 70, 73-76, 78, 82–83
LaJoie, Randy, 55
lapped, 17
leukemia, 78–79, 90
loose, 20

M

Marcis, Dave, 69
Marlin, Sterling, 57, 61
Martin, Mark, 8, 55, 82, 85–86
Martinsville Speedway, 74, 80
Mast, Rick, 46, 47
Miss Winston models, 37

N

National Association of Stock Car Auto Racing (NASCAR)
  divisions, 17
  history of, 10
  points system, 74
  types of tracks, 55
Nemecheck, Joe, 31
New Hampshire International Speedway, 57, 70, 85
North Carolina Motor Speedway (Rockingham), 27, 53, 66
North Wilksboro Speedway, 74

P

Pearson, David, 79
Penske, Roger, 27
Petty, Kyle, 37
Petty, Richard, 13, 21, 25, 34–35, 55, 89
pit, the, 18
Pittsboro, Indiana, 25
Pocono Raceway, 59, 70
pole position, 19
Pressley, Robert, 32

Q

quarter-midget racing, 22
qualifying, 18

R

Rainbow Warriors, 8, 40–41, 62, 68, 86
red flag, 16
Richmond International Raceway, 74
Rudd, Ricky, 42

S

Sacks, Greg, 8
Schrader, Ken, 47, 59–60
Southern 500, 73, 82, 84–85
Spencer, Jimmy, 73, 80
sprint car, 24
stock car
  defined, 19
  handling, 20
Stricklin, Hut, 73–74
Sullivan, Danny, 47

T
Talladega Superspeedway, 59–61, 69–71, 85
tight, 20
Trickle, Dick, 30
Tri-West High School, 25

U
United States Auto Club (USAC)
  license, 25
  Midget Series Championship, 25
  Silver Crown Championship, 25

Vallejo, California, 21
victory lane, 20

Wallace, Rusty, 40–41, 43, 55, 61, 74, 79–81, 83
Waltrip, Darrell, 45, 68
Waltrip, Michael, 31
white flag, 16
Winston Million, 73, 81–82, 84

yellow flag, 15